JELLYFISH

JELLYFISH

Fictions
By Mark McCaig

JELLYFISH
by Mark McCaig

Published by
New Bay Books
Fairhaven, Maryland
NewBayBooks@gmail.com

Design by Suzanne Shelden
Shelden Studios
Prince Frederick, Maryland
sheldenstudios@comcast.net

Cover Photo by Courtney Shelden

A Note on Type: This book is set in Garamond Premier Pro

Library of Congress
Cataloging-in-Publication Data

ISBN 979-8-9853477-0-8

Printed in the United States of America
First Edition

For Kim

"We see forms of life in the earlier history of the planet as relatively simple and undifferentiated—e.g., the amoeba and jellyfish—and thus denoted as primitive. We associate the development of 'higher' forms of life with increasing differentiation and specialization."

Don Oliver:
Education, Modernity, and Fractured Meaning (1989)

Quoted with permission of *State University of New York Press*

Foreword

Deep dives into the human character underlie Mark McCaig's fast-read glimpses of what at first blush would seem momentary absurdities. There's Pinky, who became deeply obsessed with her little toes and the fifth phalanges of all creatures. The stamp collector deeply troubled by the busyness of the USPS modern-day art, preferring the stately look that adorned envelopes decades in the past. The facial recognition practitioner who dispensed immediate names, among them Jellyfish, to a cousin, and Weasel, a lawyer on her elevator.

McCaig, a pioneering educator, presents appealing stories you can knock out any time, perhaps when you're waiting for somebody, or something. On hold with your doctor? His rapid-read takes, steeped in technology, at times relate uncomfortable truths. In "Upgrade," a 200-word rapier treatment of the cell-phone era, he contrasts the gleeful girl with her new prize at a cell phone store with the Asian girl disassembling trade-ins at a poisonous e-waste dump under the leering eyes of her oppressor.

In the best tradition of flash fiction, *Jellyfish* illuminates pains, excesses and charming realities in the human condition—all in a flash.

—William Lambrecht, Creative Director: New Bay Books

Table of Contents

PHILATELIST 1

PINKY 2

STATISTICIAN 3

HOME CURE 4

ADHERENCE TO FORM 5

FACIAL RECOGNITION 6

EMFs 7

BREATHARIAN 8

MAGAZINES 9

DIABETIC 10

CORNERS 11

FORM 12

DEEP-SEA PhD 13

QUEEN'S GUARD 14

UPGRADE 15

GRAMMARIAN 16

HEAVEN'S DOOR 17

CURATOR 18

ANGLES OF INCIDENCE 19

COLLECTOR 20

PHILATELIST

While his mother and others say he should work in the post office, he hates the mundane use of postage, especially the ubiquitous: flags, the Liberty Bell, lilies for Easter. No, odd jobs and disability checks suit him, feed his collection fine. He corresponds worldwide, affixing stamps with aviation themes. His most coveted stamp is not the black-on-magenta British Guiana one-cent, nor the Hawaiian Missionaries. No, he would only kill for the Curtiss Jenny, that of the upside-down biplane. His mother comes to the top of the basement stairs with the latest in the Nature of America series, Kelp Forest. She is not allowed beyond the second step, and she knows it. He abhors the busy landscapes. Just look how the big-eyed grouper crowds the jellyfish mashed by the kelp that leads to the seal, the shark in the distance and so on. Despicable gimmickry.

PINKY

One day the massage therapist begins treating the whole body from the feet. She pastes reflexology charts to her walls. Finding the foot too vast, she soon works only with people's pinky toes. When a friend asks why, she says the pinky-pull feels magnetic. Some clients leave. She finds a slim text, *Disorders of the Phalanges*, and commits it to memory. She legally changes her name to Pinky. Fewer clients still. She develops fierce enmity for diabetes and frostbite, little toe-killers both. From photographs on the web, she learns to identify the little toes of sixty-seven species of animals. In her free time, which is expanding, Pinky paints watercolor pinkies. She cuts holes in all of her socks just to watch her own, where she favors Foot Loose magenta polish. With her composer friend, she lays earnest plans for a pinky opera, working title *Out Here On The End.* She confides to a date that the distal phalanx has become her favorite, her specialty. In a moment of insight, she changes the spelling of her name from ending in "y" to ending in "ie," since two lower-case "i's" make the perfect pictograph for her desire to occupy the very spaces where the pinkies meet the world.

STATISTICIAN

From the day on television when he heard *3 out of 5 moms surveyed prefer Jif*, it has always been numbers. That Babe Ruth homered once out of every 11.8 at bats, that the Babe led the league with a 1.75 earned run average in 1916. The municipal sewage data he's paid to correlate flows online, so he telecommutes 4 out of 5 days. His favorite scientific quotation is Haldane's, apocryphal or not, about the Creator's *inordinate fondness for beetles*, because it relies on the numbers: 1 in 5 plant or animal species is a beetle. Despite the curiosity of meeting someone with what he could only name an inordinate fondness for 20% of her toes, his online dating success ratio has been a null set, a marked contrast, yet the logical twin to the 100% of the time he sleeps alone. His life's work has been to prove a direct correlation, a 1-to-1 ratio, between the percentage of water covering the earth and the percentage of water within the human body. He believes true understanding will include layers, fathoms if you will, wherein both corporeal and ecological imbalances will be understood and one day corrected, using his Ideal Water Number, were he to reveal it. With 542 plays (and counting) in his iTunes, his favorite song is *The Age of Aquarius* by the 5th Dimension.

HOME CURE

Of course, Vitamin C daily, and eight tumblers of distilled water. Sixty minutes cardio to lessen depression. Meat tenderizer soothes stings in the young: sweat bees, sea nettles. Cold washcloths for headache, or warm. Migraines? Ice bath by candlelight. Ginger tea settles dyspepsia. For ennui, try minor league baseball, doubleheaders preferred. Black walnut salve expels splinters. A mustard poultice can uproot even the cancer, but only from lungs, and early. Better at night, and mind you don't overdo the mustard mash and sear the skin. Cinnamon and honey dulls blemishes. Sunlight smooths melancholia. Olive oil for dry skin and hair, though some swear by coconut. Oil, that is. Elvis's peanut butter-bacon milkshake can sometimes break the blues. Best to use hickory-smoked. Tobacco for dementia, but not every damn day. A barefoot night stroll, full moon, can lift the gloom. Never a blue moon. Black haw tea calms lady problems. Hot, flat stones in a line down the back for hopelessness. Spider bites? Hard liquor, but only clear. Finally, lavender tincture on the temples stills the insomnia and consequent ruminating. That, or moonshine.

ADHERENCE TO FORM

She can't remember
when all thoughts came seventeen
syllables in size.

                    Silence itself shrank.
                    Or did it grow, just to fit
                    the beats, the three lines?

Adherence to form
corrugates every piece,
water into ice.

FACIAL RECOGNITION

The guy at the 7-Eleven register, where she buys her smokes: *Tamarind*. The lady next to her on the commuter bus: *Iceberg* (the lettuce, not the melting sea mountain). Her boss, at the NSA: *Geode*. See, she specializes in nodal points on the software team, especially the distance between the eyes and depth of the eye sockets, but she dabbles in cheekbone shapes and jawlines. Secretly, she gives herself ten seconds to name people by their faces. Lawyer in the elevator: *Weasel*. Her gyno: *Napoleon* (the nose/lips combo). The last man she slept with: *Sarsparilla*. Don't ask. At times it's a curse, like on subways or at the Portrait Gallery. Her cousin from Jersey, the first she named: *Jellyfish*. Toasting s'mores at camp, the firelight shimmering across her face, she just knew. Her mother: *Rosemary* (the spice she dislikes). Her brother, the stamp collector, not just because of the beard: *Grizzly*. Starbucks dude: *Foxface*. Because she distrusts reflections, she cannot, will not name herself. Faceless dreams yield no names whatsoever. Once, a lady at a red light became her most accurate ever, both for her cruciform nasal-ocular proportions and for an aspect of hopefulness in her sideways glance: *Rosary*.

EMFs

Talk about great cell service: a hundred-fifty feet up, karabiner clipped to rail atop the tower, he gets all the bars logging in to measure signal rates on the clustered gray and white boxes. Might as well check his fantasy team while he waits. Need to trade for another QB since his got concussed. *Ka-ching.* Payroll just dropped. Not bad for a high school grad. Probably got time for a smoke up here. Signals all good, but gotta clean the birdshit from the Sprint box. Why is it always Sprint? Man, he hates crows. *Ding.* Text from his mom: *Where are you?* Should he lie? She writes like a thousand letters a week about the hazards of electromagnetic fields, even bought this high-end EMF detector from Amazon that she hauls around with her flyers in that damn canvas bag. Libraries, preschools, hell, everywhere, sure we're all gonna get cancer. Cell dings again: *Where are you?* He stubs his Marlboro on the iron ladder, enjoys the spin when he chucks it. He unlocks the karabiner, then down, always sure one hand and foot contact a rung, just to be on the safe side.

BREATHARIAN

Vegetarian, she declares. Harmless enough. Craving ever less, her limits escalate—gluten-free, soy-free, dairy-free. She reads radical magazines from Glut, her food co-op, savoring how the scents of patchouli and falafel mix when she turns the pages. Sitting on her organic futon, one day she finds the answer: spirulina. Yes. Time slows. In the mirror, changes—what she considers a fierce clarity emerges in her bone structure, even as her thoughts detach. Her eyes pop, those of a caught fish. She begins whistling, praying more. Near the end, she often opens her empty fridge, admiring the beckoning whiteness, ignoring the tug from her gut. Her last friend finds what remains of her, heart stopped, lightarian, released from all of this, her ultimate vision not the sun-speckled kelp forest, as planned, but a meat lover's pizza, sausage and pepperoni gleaming with grease.

MAGAZINES

From *Psychology Today*, he knows all about OCD and agoraphobia, still he is the person he is, and he accepts himself (*Shambala Sun*). He marks his passage through time by *Time's* Man of the Year and the *Sports Illustrated* Swimsuit Issue, by *US News and World Report's* Best Colleges and Universities, even by *Vogue's* Fall Fashion. He thinks he understands a bit about devotion, at night. Moths patter the yellow porch bulb. Inside, he delays the cellophaned latest issue while he eats his Hungry Man in front of the nightly news, his dessert and decaf in front of *Jeopardy!*, all the while savoring the articles that await, and never, not once, obsessing. This putting off, the subsequent release into the pages, could this be love?

DIABETIC

She looks behind her: the ten thousand biohazards, the gallons of sicksweet urine, the hundred apologies to the husband and kids, and yes, the clear days as well. She looks ahead at more of the same, only really, more clear than not. She does that, she revises her thoughts about it. She writes more poems on it than love, looking up synonyms for *always*, for *acceptance*, for *rage*, for *sweet*. She pretends not to worry about complications. When does chronic become obsessed? Five endocrinologists. No, six. Six, the same number as the supplements she takes at night: fish oil, 5HTP, women's daily, alpha lipoic acid, garlic, an Ayurvedic blend for glucose control, wild bitter melon. Okay, seven. She counts things. Three times, her Medic Alert bracelet has broken, and this seems darkly absurd. She smiles way less than before, and teaches herself to force it. She wore an amber necklace early on, some folk remedy, until the string broke, and even now she can hear the clatter, followed by beads rolling across the pinewood floor.

CORNERS

He carries the honing tools into the jobsite half an hour early. Six beers at lunch, humping drywall one day at a time, so he sharpens mornings only, ahead of the dulling Budweiser. Even the micro-dust from the Salvadoran finishers sanding mud over the tape can soften the 90s. He takes the worn hasp from his tool belt, files a metal corner seam, takes out the square to check the angle, then resumes filing. The shavings settle on the ancient, hopelessly unsquare oak floor planks. How do carpenters abide such fault? Downing the dregs of his coffee, he looks across the silent site: Naked bulbs illuminate the countless seams and metal studs beckoning to be perfected. Hearing the first truck door slam, the shit-talking on King Street below, he takes solace in the only useful thing he remembers from algebra: how a graph can approach the axes infinitely and never reach congruence, never once match the mythical ninety degrees at the vertex.

FORM

Slow, green mantis prays:
her eyes refract fifty-fold,
hidden wings ready.

DEEP-SEA PhD

She taps her wedding band on the super-thick porthole, platinum on plexiglass. Only seven hours at a time in the alien deep-sea biosphere, but between flying to Tasmania, dive-team meetings and post-dive debrief, a solid week away from arguing with him. A scientist, she disdains irony, yet here she chuckles at the fact of her *going down* while he perhaps does the same back home with his little grad assistant. Her doctoral thesis explored reproduction in the *ctenophora*, the predatory, multiple-lobed comb jellies known for their rainbow iridescence in light, for their bioluminescence in darkness. These are hermaphroditic, capable of propagation and continuance without mates. So much simpler that way. As they enter the bone-cold "twilight zone," she watches the submersible's spotlights rainbow a numberless school, admiring even the coincidence of the silent "c" that begins the word *ctenophore*, how it mirrors the silence in the sea itself, and in the descending sub, save for her ring's steady, hushed tapping, tapping.

QUEEN'S GUARD

Big Tree this week in Turlock, then down to Campos Brothers in Caruthers. His bees: the world's most numerous biker gang, half a million tiny hogs rumbling through the air towards the lush lines of almond trees. If they had tiny leather vests, Queen's Guard lettering their backs. People always ask about getting stung, but it's all about the gear, you know? After three seasons, he knows the deal. The greenies gripe about all the water for the trees, what with the drought, sometimes carry signs out front when his bee trucks roll in. Tell it to the consumer, he says. Supply and demand. Colony collapse, now that's a problem. He ignores the buzz in his pocket when his girl, back home, texts from her new phone, probably to remind him about night-school homework. She can wait. After all the unloading, this, this is his moment: when they all zoom off for the pink buds, leaving the queens alone in their hives, waiting for the pollen, for the horde's droning, encircling return.

UPGRADE

A teenage girl pushes into the glossy showroom, dragging her mother. The slick-haired salesman has led the wireless store in volume six out of the last nine months. In a drawer at home, he stores a collection of his discards, naming each for the girl whose voice had filled its speaker the most: His blue, belt-clip Nokia is his ex, *Gina*; the Razr is *Felicia*; and his first flip goes by happy-hour *Lulu*. Noting the mother's platinum-set, chunky diamond, he shills the new G4 touch-screen, and soon she signs the family plan contract, skimming the fine print. The girl's first text: *OMG I got an iPhone!* After a tech transfers her contacts, she drops her pink Samsung in the box marked with the green recycling logo.

A week later, back it ships to China, crated with some two thousand others. In an outdoor junkyard another girl rips the pink off, then bathes the phone's guts in hydrochloric acid. She strips gold, copper, iridium. Her hands bear scars, and her blood flows toxic like the village river. Under a blue tarp, her chain-smoking boss sometimes keeps his eye on more than precious metals. Her secret? She can hear voices—mostly speaking in English—coming from the old phones.

GRAMMARIAN

She places the phone in its cradle, forgetting—correction—*disregarding* her grown daughter's cursing. Hadn't she first thanked her for the card, then merely rectified her common error? It's "thank you for myriad things," not "thank you for *a* myriad *of* things." Strunk and White #16: *Omit needless words.* A stack of essays beckons anyway, personal reflections, no less. Why not just invite more comma splices? Retired, still a couple night school sections a year. From her immaculate desk she marks the ongoing demise of proper usage: non-parallel structure, subject-verb disagreement, passive voice, uninspired diction. Despite her handouts, commas still mystify them, and semicolons? Forget it. Her wall clock chimes the half hour. Like others who safeguard the rules, she begins her litany of blame with cell phones. *So fucking snarky, Mom.* Of course, the second adjective is considered "informal," but she lets that pass. Profanity, though, bespeaks vulgarity, laziness. Her red felt attacks, squeaking.

HEAVEN'S DOOR

The door opens with that children's choir version, after the Dunblane massacre, for its context. She buys the CD, the least she can do, cries in her car between work and home. Random, really, hearing next on BIG 97.5 the original Dylan wrote for *Pat Garret* and *Billy the Kid*, enthralled by its brevity, its reverb. After someone in a pub tells her about all the cover versions, she starts filling her racks, later her hard drive. Soon, video clips: Dylan with his Rolling Thunder Revue, Clapton on the Old Grey Whistle Test, all rasta style, Springsteen showing up at a café in Berlin. *Klopf, klopf, klopfen an die Himmelstür.* If she did ever invite someone to join her annual viewing marathon, she'd open with the very first: badge-wearing Slim Pickens shot in the gut, having the sense to stagger to a riverbank to catch one last sunset, and his woman, there but keeping her distance from that long black cloud. And her finale would have to be Warren Zevon, metastatic, improvising, like we all will: *Open up, open up, open up for me…cause I'm knockin' on heaven's door.*

CURATOR

She straps on her Optivisor to magnify the moon jelly tentacles arrayed on her worktable, flicks its LED lamp. To address widespread delamination in the replica, she has removed, cleaned, and arranged each of one hundred sixty-three translucid glass ribbons, touching them only with her tweezers, careful to preserve their order clockwise around the medusa. Adagio Mozart pulsates through her earbuds. For cleaning, white spirit, its mineral scent. In most, the archival glue offers little resistance. Most. Micro-painting begins today to fill in the chips from sloppy storage, from time. The paint department names the glittering color for *Aurelia aurita* "peach melba." Her daydreams undulate from gliding in an oblivious school of jellies to dropping the entire *Sea Creatures in Glass* down the open museum stairwell in a crystal crash. Ringed by the enhanced, rippling strips, she discovers drift.

ANGLES OF INCIDENCE

His one true ambition? To see the green flash just after sunset, just before sunrise. Preparing for the microseconds, he trains his eyes with minute daily exercises: focus close in, focus far, clock on the wall, oak leaf outside, clock, leaf, clock, leaf, clock, leaf, until he feels strain in the tiny muscles that regulate aperture. He is rubbing his eyes, post-exercise, the moment his wife stands in the living room, suitcase in hand, having had enough. Although he disagrees with her regarding the usefulness of metaphor, once in his car while speeding home to catch another sunset, a distant thunderhead pulsed, and intermittently it resembled, he thought, a sea nettle, the jade species he'd seen snorkeling on their honeymoon. Such refracted light. And when the slightest suggestion of that green from the faraway storm hit his retinas, he focused on it, out the driver's side window, thinking maybe this would suffice, this luminosity, were he never to see the green flash. Maybe this afterglow would ease the sting. Thinking this, all the while, knowing that.

About the Author

COLLECTOR

He began with fossil shark teeth as a boy, each sharp trace from the Miocene he still finds a small miracle, a mystery tumbling with the shoreline pebbles onto the hometown beach he walks this morning. The author often assembles his words from a lifetime on the western shore of the Chesapeake, whether scoping migrant birds in sunlight or celestial bodies by night. Naked-eye observations, say of the Andromeda galaxy or of Hooded Mergansers cruising the saltmarsh, thrill him most. He keeps amateur lists of these and other natural phenomena. A lifelong teacher, he cofounded a democratic school over two decades ago with his wife, who, along with his two grown daughters, remains the dearest treasure he's found in a lifetime of gathering. He's written four books now, from poetry to nonfiction to this, his first fiction. The different sets of words between the covers, he thinks, resemble curio cabinets, relics of various stages, so he keeps writing to relive the collector's first rush of discovery. Although the longer he lives, the less he seems to know—and he counts this as progress—he appreciates each generous reader to the point where words vanish, like the keening Tundra Swans come spring.